ONE WAY

www.pictureshowpress.net

Cover image: Jeff Giniewicz, istockphoto.com

FIRST EDITION

"Dance With Me" was previously published as a novel
excerpt with {stet}, the creative writing journal of UT
Arlington's English Department.

ISBN-13: 978-1-7324144-3-3
ISBN-10: 1-7324144-3-2

ONE
WAY

Mohammed Sumili

Picture Show Press

Content

1   Suspect

7   Dance With Me

21   One Way

29   Merciless Bastard

35   The Matchmaker

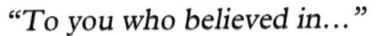

"To you who believed in…"

Suspect

I was woken up one Friday by Janet, the building manager.
She was gently poking me. I slowly opened one of my eyes
and closed it again. Then I opened the other one to confirm
it was her. However, when I heard her mention the police,
my eyes blinked like a flickering light bulb before I opened
them wide. With the lovely Sheridan Smith out of my head, I
was able to steadily gaze at Janet's freckled face with
bewilderment.

"A policeman wants to speak to you," she said with a sly
look of suspicion in her eyes.

What on earth would the police want from me? I asked
myself. I dashed out of my room and found a tall, bald-
headed man waiting for me. He wore a black suit.

"Hiya." I was trying to fake an English accent. He
greeted me with a gloomy smile. He apologized for the
disturbance, which I thought was unjustifiable. Janet was

behind me. She seemed glad like a puppy that had flushed a bird out of the bushes on its first hunting season. I asked if there was a problem. He told me that he wanted to check some details with me.

"Could you give me five minutes to prepare myself?" I asked. I immediately dashed into the restroom, and washed my face and hair as if I had been attacked by a drunk skunk. Being aware that I wasn't entirely dreaming, I gathered my thoughts and stepped out into the kitchen area.

In the kitchen, he properly introduced himself. His name was Ralph. Again, he apologized for Janet's behaviour. I didn't know what to make of her behaviour, but my friend, Nizar, would describe it as being horrendous, a word he recently picked up. I offered him tea, but he declined. While I was making tea for myself, a few drops of water fell from my dripping hair into the cup. I wanted to make a new one, but I thought Ralph would suspect I was nervous. So I forced myself to take a few sips of it during my chat with him.

I had to answer a few questions regarding my stay in England, which didn't bother me at all, but he finally pissed me off when he clumsily said, "I didn't know there were so many Saudis living in Exeter!"

I wanted to ask him if he had a problem with that, but I thought it would be saner to avoid being confrontational. Then he asked me about the 7th of July, which explained this unexpected visit. Because a group of dickheads had blown up a train, I, the law-abiding citizen, was to be suspected. It really made me feel unwanted. I am glad I didn't mix it up with the 4th of July, which has a more explosive ring to it.

Anyhow, he asked me if I had encountered any racial problems of any kind. What a stupid question. Well, the way in which this visit came about could be an appropriate start.

"Not at all," I answered. "The English people showed a

remarkable way of dealing with the incident. They are truly a civilized nation." Yeah, sure. Last week, a Muslim woman complained that a man had shouted at her at a bus stop. He rudely told her to go back from where she had come. None of the people there had tried to back him off. Usually, they would say he had problems (Doesn't everyone have problems?), or that it was a matter for the police to deal with.

After Ralph left, Christina, my Taiwanese flatmate, asked me about it. She was a nice girl, but she would be thinking about this a lot. As a matter of fact, she once told me that she used to dream that I would abduct her and chop her head off while shouting *Allahu akbar*, like a terrorist in Iraq. Now where the hell did she get an idea like that from? I wouldn't be surprised if she thought about moving out after Ralph's visit.

In the afternoon, I went to the mosque. It was a nice sunny day. I really liked summer in England. Roses, in different sizes and shapes, bloomed everywhere.

I met Nizar after prayer. I told him about the police and he was annoyed, too.

"It's horrendous!" he exploded. "No, no, it's a horrendous act of racial profiling." I tried to calm him down, especially since he, as usual, was overreacting. I told him that Ralph was courteous and that he had smiled the whole time.

"He was smiling, you say?!" Nizar continued as we walked to Sidwell Street. "Boy, you're a nice guy. Have you ever asked yourself why the English people smile? I mean, do they smile because they really want to or because they are forced to? Let me tell you one thing about these people, bro. Deep inside themselves, they think we are nothing but a bunch of despicable narrow-minded terrorists who came to live among them."

"Come on, that's not a polite thing to say," I objected.

3

"I don't care! What else did he ask you about?"

"The London bombings. What I thought about them."

"See? What did I tell you?" Nizar launched into a rant as we nipped through a narrow footpath. "Why is your opinion of importance to them now? Why didn't it matter before? I mean, when they went to war in Iraq."

"What in the hell has Iraq to do with what we are talking about now?" I interrupted. "The guy visited me, asked some questions, and left. I don't see any problem with that. If you have one, you can say it to them when they visit you. You can even tell them 'no' if you want."

"Do you think I'm stupid?"

"Why are you saying that now? Afraid, huh?"

"Not at all," he said with a smile. "It is as simple as this: If I say no, they will obviously drag me to their station, beat the hell out of me, lock me in a dirty cellar with a sack on my head, and piss on me whenever they want. And when everybody finds out, a no good-for-nothing drug addict will go on TV apologizing, describing what happened as *horrendous*, saying that the people who had done it don't represent the majority of the English people."

I was going to respond to Nizar when we came face-to-face with a terrifying beast that I thought only existed in Disneyland, but it happened to be real—it was a Scooby Doo dog, and it stood right in front of the door of the Duke of York pub at the corner of Sidwell Street.

I glanced back at Nizar, who had suddenly vanished. Seconds later, I heard him calling me from the other side of the street. How did he get there? I couldn't be bothered to know at that moment. I was there alone, face-to-face with a gigantic, flea-harbouring beast. It was like a showdown in one of those western movies.

The dog advanced towards me; I, on the other hand, stood quivering. My heart thumped rapidly. I had two options. I could slowly turn back and run as fast as I could, or I could jump the beast, hold it by the neck, bite its nose, and pluck its eyes out before it cut me to pieces. However, people would consider that brutality because I would be torturing the poor, beastly creature.

All of that cleared when I realized that the ferocious beast was half a metre away from me. It stared me in the eyes, its mouth disgustingly drooling. It released a horrifying growl as if it was telling me that it was ready. It took one step forward, and I took two steps backwards.

The chase was about to launch when a chubby, middle-aged Englishman came out of the pub. He was holding a pint of beer in his hand. He stood leaning to one side of the pub's door, blocking the other side with his huge belly. He called the dog. At first, it ignored him, but the man, after gulping some beer, said with authority, "Come on, boy!"

I didn't know the reason that made him call that beast 'boy,' but the dog finally listened to the man. It took a quick look back at him, gazed at me, and released another growl. Then it lifted one of its rear legs, urinated on the pavement right in front of me, and went inside the pub. The man smiled at me and went in after it.

I crossed to the other side of the street and argued with Nizar because he hadn't alerted me to the dog. On our way to the cathedral, where we usually had coffee at a nearby cafe, Nizar kept talking about his loathing of dogs. I didn't pay attention to what he was saying. My mind was busy trying to figure out the sincerity of the English people's smile.

Dance With Me

After classes were over, I rushed towards the train station. I got a ticket to Plymouth, which wasn't expensive. I dashed to the platform because the train was to leave in five minutes.

"Excuse me sir, is this the train going to Plymouth?" I asked a man wearing a suit. He nodded with a smile.

On the train I phoned Kate and told her that I was on my way. I sat beside a chubby girl who was reading a book about losing weight. There was a packet of doughnuts and a can of soft drink. It seemed that she was sticking to every point mentioned in the book. I pulled out *The Catcher in the Rye* by Salinger and started reading, a habit I had picked up here. My English teacher back home suggested that I should read the book because it would give me an insight into American youth culture.

I really miss talking to Dr. Saleem. He was an understanding person. I learned a lot from him. However, I couldn't understand the reason why he insisted on teaching us *Animal Farm*. Too bad he was to leave the department. Every time I asked why, he would comment that there were things I'd know with time.

I figured he couldn't take it anymore; he had been furiously attacked by other faculty members who didn't appreciate his way of teaching. "He is corrupting the student minds," they would claim. I recalled a discussion that happened one day between Dr. Saleem and Ayed, a student with a long beard and thick rimless glasses who always sat in the front row. They disagreed on something related to communism and Ayed kept repeating: "It is against the teaching of Islam!" Dr. Saleem settled the argument by glaring and telling him that he wanted to get on with class.

"Ali, they don't want to teach anything here!" he would protest every time I went to meet him in his office hours.

"Yeah, Doctor, when in Rome do as the Romans do," I would reply.

To tell the truth, I don't blame him. The twelve years he had spent in the States must have influenced his way of thinking. He didn't expect that everybody would object to his ideas, especially to the ones related to women.

In one of his office hours, I told him of my intention of taking a language course abroad. He told me I was wasting my money. I just sat looking at him, my eyes blinking.

"Don't misunderstand me," he said. "Look at it from this angle. You'll be studying for eight weeks, right?"

I nodded quickly.

"Good," he continued, "It will take you at least a month to get used to the new environment there. By the time you start to get along well, you will find that you're supposed to leave. I think it isn't worth it. Unless you'll be staying no less than six months, you won't be able to gain that much. Trust me, it is a waste of money. Yet if you want to consider it a recreational tour under the disguise of studying, that is something else." He winked shrewdly when he said those last words.

"Tickets, please," the train manager said in his sharp voice, interrupting my reading. I hadn't managed to finish reading the second paragraph of the first page. I gave him the ticket which he punched with an instrument he was holding. The girl beside me gave the man her ticket, stretching her hand in front of me. I noticed a small, white bandage on her shoulder. It skipped out of my mind and I didn't know what it was called although I'd seen it on a TV commercial.

When the manager returned the ticket to the girl, she, accidentally, dropped the pack of doughnuts. I picked it up and gave it back to her. She smiled and thanked me; her smile exposed her yellow teeth which, then, explained the bandage on the shoulder.

Luckily, the girl got off at the next station and I sat in her warm seat. I wanted to sit beside the window. I stopped reading the book and sat gazing out the window. I enjoyed observing nature. I think it is the only beauty that has been left unspoiled nowadays. The tall trees, the green meadows, and the sea. Allah's heavens on his earth. I wondered if I could stroll around those meadows one day.

The train reached Plymouth after about an hour and ten minutes. The station was crowded with people. I had to pass through security. Being aware of what to do, I didn't make a fool of myself. I met Kate at the entrance. She was wearing a sleeveless white top and a short jean skirt. I liked her legs, proportioned above the knees. We shook hands and off we went.

"How was the trip?"

"Nice. I didn't know that Plymouth was near."

"Well, now that you know, you can come here whenever you have the time."

Plymouth was bigger than Exeter. The buildings were

modern. The city centre was remarkable. We sat in a coffee shop and chatted for a while.

"So how are your studies?"

"Not bad, what about yours?"

"Don't ask. I'm getting fed up with analysing data. Luckily, my super is away for a couple of days which means getting some time off, hooray!"

"That sounds good."

"So how are your friends?"

"Oh, they're fine."

"What about you?"

"What about me?"

We were interrupted by the waitress who brought our orders; iced mocha for Kate and a cappuccino for me.

"Did you manage to make any close friendships with any of your classmates?" she asked. Her lips, covered with a fair lipstick, gently sucked at the straw.

"I don't get you."

She smiled at me and asked if I had managed to get a girlfriend or not. If it were my friend, Nizar, I would have told him to fuck off.

"Not yet. I don't think girls would be interested in me."

"Oh, don't say that. I'm sure you'll get a girl soon. You're a nice guy," she said, patting my hand.

I tried to change the subject because stupid ideas started forming in my head. I asked about Plymouth and the reason it was more modern than Exeter. Kate informed me about World War II and that the city was bombed during that time.

"It was flattened," she said, irritated. "Nazi bastards!"

I didn't understand the last part. However, I noticed she didn't ask me about her mum, whose homestay I was living in. She took me for a tour around the city centre, then we took the bus to the seaside.

The seaside was crowded with people. There were many

cafés. I liked the sculptures there, some of them signified times of war. Some of the sculptures had the names of soldiers inscribed on them. Interestingly, I read names like Ahmad. Muslim names. I pondered for a while over that. How could one die for a country that isn't his? I asked myself. I didn't bother to find an answer. The seaside wasn't like Exeter. There weren't a lot of half-naked girls. Kate and I drank a couple of fresh drinks and strolled back to her apartment.

"Next time, come early and I'll take you to the aquarium," she said as we walked again by the sculptures.

It took us around twenty minutes to get to her flat. It was a nice flat. There was another student sharing it with Kate. Kate's room was large. It had a built-in wardrobe, a dressing table, a double bed, and a study desk. There was a mirror on the dressing table and there was also a nice collection of creams and perfumes. Kate sat on the leather chair beside the desk and I sat on the bed.

I liked the way she arranged her books and papers on the desk; books on the left side of the laptop and papers on the right. There were some photos of her, taken with some friends, stapled to a notice board on the wall. I also saw the photo we had taken in Exeter. She was smiling in her bathing suit. I, however, was standing looking at the photographer. I had been embarrassed because my arm was around Kate's waist. Bob had told me to do it. I had failed to fake a smile.

"Would you like anything to drink?" she asked before turning on the stereo.

"No thanks. But can I use the loo, please?"

"Of course you can!"

She went outside the room and came back with a small plastic jug. "I know you prefer to wash with water," she said, winking at me.

We went out for dinner after we watched TV in the small kitchen. On the way out, I was curious about a box that was left at the entrance of the flat.

"What's in it?"

"Oh, it's Bob's. He said he would pick it up later this week."

"I thought you broke up."

"We did, but that doesn't mean we can't speak to each other."

I just shrugged. "Why did you break up?"

It seemed that Kate didn't want to answer my naïve question. She was shuffling the key in the keyhole. I didn't know what made me ask such a question.

She smiled at me. "It's a long story. I don't want to bother you with it."

"Sorry about that. It isn't my business, please forgive me."

"Ah, don't worry about it."

We ate at an Indian restaurant. Kate had a cheeseburger and I had chicken tikka with rice. We chatted as we ate.

"So when will the last train to Exeter leave?" Kate asked, after swallowing a chunk of her burger.

"Well," I said, mixing the curry with the rice. "There's one at twenty past nine and another one at twelve. I'll think I'll take the first."

"Great! We've still got time to go to some places," she said, taking another chunk.

I insisted on paying for the meal. Kate didn't like it. She was also pressing to pay for her own meal. To avoid any misunderstanding, I told her it was a cultural custom. Always blame it on the culture.

"In that case, it's all right," she accepted.

The weather was cool outside. The breeze tickled my face as I stepped out. Kate took me to a pub. It was modern compared to the ones in Exeter. The place was also a nightclub and restaurant. The building was constructed mostly out of glass. Because it was early, the place wasn't stuffed with people. It had an upper floor where people danced. However, according to Kate, there were two DJs playing different types of music on each floor. People in the pub were drinking and gossiping. Some sat around tables, while others were standing in groups, swaying with the music.

I followed Kate, who maneuvered her way to the bar. People were queuing; the beautiful bartenders served the orders with skilled swiftness. Everything was neat, except for the smell of vomit that seemed to have been swept up a while ago. The floor was wet and sticky. The smell annoyed me, but the people queuing weren't bothered—maybe because they were too drunk to notice it.

"What will you have? A coke as usual?" Kate asked, raising her voice.

"No, I think I'll have a bottle of Corona."

"When did you start drinking?" she asked, smiling.

"Three weeks ago," I replied.

I fumbled in my pockets to pay for the drink, but Kate said she was going to pay. I told her that I drank it with lime. We sat and talked about my adventurous step into the drinking world. I had already prepared an excuse. I told her that I was looking for an experience.

"Well, don't go too far with it," she said, gulping from her glass of gin.

Kate flicked her fingers to the music while I tapped my feet. A group of girls started dancing. Then some men joined them. One of the girls was slim. She was wearing a short, white mini skirt and a red top. She was the target of the men's attention. I sat observing her as I drank my second bottle.

"Do you think she's hot?"

"No," I answered, turning quickly to Kate.

"Why?!"

"She is thin."

"But men like slim girls."

"Well, where I come from a curvy girl is a nice catch."

"I'm glad to hear that. It sounds encouraging. I shouldn't worry about losing weight then." We exchanged smiles.

"So do you hang out at clubs with your friends?" she asked.

"Yeah, we go to Timepiece a lot."

"Not bad, do you like dancing?"

I smiled. Embarrassed, I told her that I didn't know how to dance.

"What? You're in England and you haven't started dancing yet?"

I sat quietly.

"You should try."

"I did, but I think I look silly."

"Bullshit. Anyone can dance, you just need a little practice."

"I know but my body is… it's…" I lost the word I was trying to say.

"You mean stiff?"

"Yes."

"That's because you don't dance."

The DJ put on a song by Shakira. Kate pulled me to the dance floor. Her body moved swiftly as she danced. I stood looking at her. She told me to move my feet. I tried to force them, but they were chained together. I remembered Saud's words when I first started dancing. "You look pathetic," he had commented in the postgraduate centre. I didn't dance after that.

Kate held my hands and moved me around. She told me to follow her lead. Salsa, they called it. I stepped on her feet several times, and she laughed when I did so. Another song started. The lyrics went, *I wanna dance with somebody.*

Kate's moves became slow. She was looking sexier. Her eyes were drowsy. She stepped close to me. I continued to look at her, hypnotised by her eyes. I stepped close to her. I raised my hand towards her waist, but stopped. Noticing that, she smiled at me and took my hands and placed them around her waist. Then she wrapped her hands around my neck. I felt my heart thumping rapidly. A shiver went through my spine. Sweat formed on my skin. Her chest brushed against mine. I was finally dancing, but not with any girl, it was with Kate. I wanted to lean and kiss her lips, but the song ended.

We went back to the table. She said I was okay for a beginner. I apologised for stamping on her feet.

"It always happens at the beginning," she said. Actually, we had to yell at each other because of the music. I glanced at my watch and noticed that the train was going to leave in five minutes.

"I'm going to miss the train," I yelled, pointing to my watch.

"You can't make it, it's too late. The station is a ten-minute walk from here and your bag is in the flat. Take the other one," she yelled.

We drank again. I had four bottles. R&B music was on. People trooped to the dance floor. Kate and I followed. I danced energetically. I didn't know why. Could it be the drink, or because there was no Saud to make fun of me? I danced with Kate who became wild and sexier. We nodded our heads and shook our bums. But I still felt nervous every time she got close to me. She turned, her back towards me. I danced close to her. My heart started thumping again, sweat forming; our bodies merged again. My hands were on her waist. As her body brushed against mine, I felt an erection. I immediately pulled away from her. I pointed to my watch to show that it was time to go.

"Okay. Wait, I want to go to the ladies' room," she said. Her lips wet my ear.

We left at a quarter to twelve. I told Kate she should stay and that I could take a taxi, but she insisted on accompanying me to the station. We hurried to the station.

At the train station, Kate bid me farewell. I was going to shake her hand, but she embraced me and planted a kiss on my cheek. I just patted her back.

"Text me when you reach Exeter, okay?" Kate said, waving at me as I rushed to the train that was leaving in ten minutes.

It was rather quiet. There weren't many people on the platform. I asked one of the staff if it was the train that was headed to Exeter. He affirmed this with a smile.

"You can get on at the rear," he said. I looked at him. He then pointed to the back of the train, towards which I hurried.

The compartment I sat in seemed quiet. There weren't many passengers. There was a man with trim hair, sleeping. A middle-aged woman with ruffled grey hair sat in front of me. A group of teenagers, three boys and a girl, were at the back. I noticed a couple of suitcases left on the seats on the row beside me. Probably they belonged to someone who was using the toilet, I thought. But I spotted two bodies tucked in sleeping bags. Low class people, I supposed. A girl with dark blue jeans and a black pullover came after me. She sat at the front.

After a while, the train manager came to check the tickets. He approached the girl first. She didn't have a ticket and told him that she would like to buy one. She bought it following the same polite procedures the English take. The 'Thank you, cheers' thing.

I checked my pocket for my ticket. The manager approached the sleeping man. I could clearly see the features of the manager. He was a chubby fellow, reddish cheeks. He wore a turquoise suit. He gently spoke to the man.

"Tickets, please."

But the sleeping man didn't respond.

"Tickets, please," the manager repeated in his squeaking voice.

Again there was no response. The manager gently knocked with his metal keys on the wooden table that was in front of the sleeping man. He knocked twice. But the man was still sound asleep. The manager's eyes widened and he knocked hard on the table and said in an irritated voice: "Tickets please!"

The man, I thought, must have come from a far place, which would explain his deep sleep. After several attempts, the man finally woke up. The manager asked him for the tickets. But the man didn't have one. When he was asked if he wanted to buy one, it turned out that he didn't have any money. The manager, who was holding to his patience, told him that he "was off the train." But the man sat in his seat.

"You're off," repeated the manager, stiffening.

The man stood, rambling some words. He was tall. Yet he was staggering. Drunk? Or maybe on drugs? He got his guitar from the upper storage rack. But he dropped it. It made him enraged.

"You fucking bastard! You'll fucking pay for it!" the man insulted the manager, who was standing in the area between the two compartments.

The man then attacked the manager with the guitar. The manager, alert, shut the glass door to avoid the hit. But the man didn't give up. It seemed that he held a grudge against the manager. He attacked him again. The guitar got caught in the door. The manager hit the door, breaking the guitar handle. The man became more furious and attacked the manager. The two of them clasped each other and staggered their way, swaying, to the second compartment.

All of that happened and nobody thought of giving the poor manager a hand. The lady in front of me was looking in all directions. She paced forwards and backwards. She asked in a trembling voice how she could get help. I didn't know the way they do that here. With panic, she felt beside her seat

17

until she finally pulled a handle above her seat. The girl with the dark jeans rushed out of the train, calling for help.

Seconds later, two members of staff came. They pinned the man down. A woman was shouting at the man: "Do you want me to use this on you?" Maybe she was threatening him with one of those electric sticks used on criminals.

"He started it! He started it!" The man wept like a child. All that fuss and the teenagers at the back were asking who caught who, as if it were a school fight.

While the fight was taking place, the two sleeping bags started to move. Like cocoons, they were opened to reveal two lovely girls. One was blonde and the other had brownish hair. I guessed from the language they spoke that they were from Eastern Europe. *Cheap labour,* I said to myself.

A drunkard—unemployed, the government paying for his expenses—was causing trouble. He was trying to snatch a free lift on a train. While, on the other hand, two hard working girls sleeping on the floor had to pay. They might be delayed for an important flight because of his act, a citizen of a civilised nation. The irony of fate.

A man in a suit, with combed grey hair, came up onto the train. He apologetically informed us that the train would be delayed. I phoned Liz and told that I would be home late.

"Oh dear!" was her reply when I told her about the incident. I also phoned Kate.

"Are you all right?" she asked, worried.

"I'm fine. No need to panic."

"Do you want me to come to the station?"

"That's kind of you, but really there is no need for that."

"You can spend the night here and leave in the morning."

Sleeping in Kate's room. I had never thought of that. Spending the night with the woman I was dancing and drinking with.

"Thanks, Kate. I really don't want to bother you. They

said it's only a twenty-minute delay." I ended the call.

While waiting for the other manager to arrive, I listened to the other passengers. The two girls beside me were explaining to each other what they could make out about what had happened. The blonde girl did most of the talking.

"Tick, tick," she said, knocking on the table. The teenagers at the back seemed to not care less about what had happened. Instead, they were talking about Hannibal and some Dr. Satan. They exchanged positive comments about their topics. The girl said loudly that she admired a scene with a chainsaw. I wished I knew what the hell they were talking about.

Another member of staff came and apologised again for the delay and informed us that another train manager was on the way and that the train would be moving within twenty-five minutes. He also mentioned that the police were on their way. One of the teenagers, out of warm concern, kindly asked about the assaulted manager's condition.

"He's had a slight injury to the head," the man said, "but he is still breathing and on his way to the hospital."

The police came and checked where the man was sitting. I saw them put a couple of things into plastic bags. They asked questions of the two ladies, who were sitting close to where the drunkard sat, and it was over. What interested me was that they had carried out their work smiling. Also, I found the lady officer attractive, her blonde hair and erect back.

It was a while before the train was on the move to Exeter. I sat in my seat, observing the darkness of the night. Nobody asked about the tickets after that. I pulled my notebook from the bag and jotted down the following thoughts:

unemployment + alcohol + free money = trouble

hunger + poverty + frustration= cheap labour

Then I let my thoughts take me adrift. I thought of Kate, the way she danced with me, her smiles, and most of all her kiss perfumed with the smell of gin.

One Way

It was a calm night. The stars shone in the dark sky. I stood in the vicinity of our house, contemplating the metamorphosis that had taken place while I was away. The house that had sheltered me for twenty-one years was not there. The rooms, whose roofs were my only respite unto which I climbed whenever I felt distress, had vanished. Many concrete pillars, with protruding iron rods, had been erected in their place. A three-story building was to be built. A five-bedroom apartment was to be my share in it. Father had finally yielded to mother's constant requests to build a big house for their seven children.

Everything was changing; things were no more the same. A new age was approaching with its own distinguishing features. I observed my car, a 2002 white Toyota Camry, at the front gate. It, too, was transformed. I didn't recognize it when I first saw it.

"What do you want?" Hassan, my younger brother, interrupted me with his loud voice. He was a tall, handsome fellow with an erect body. Since I went to England, he had developed a repulsive ego. I used to beat him up, but now he could overthrow me with ease.

"I want you to drive me to Samtah," I replied in a composed manner.

"Now?!"

"Yes."

"What for?"

"Grandfather wants a ticket to Riyadh."

"Can't it wait until tomorrow?"

"I believe you know your grandfather when he wants something."

True, grandfather was the type of person who became annoyingly demanding when he wanted anything to be done. He had called me about twelve times regarding the matter. He had had a heart operation last January and he had an appointment at a hospital in Riyadh.

"Why don't you take the car then?" Hassan asked impatiently, scratching his recently shaved chin. He was right, yet I wasn't keen on driving anymore. It seemed that my stay in the UK made me enjoy sitting in the passenger's seat.

"Let's go! If it was one of your friends, you'd be happy about it. Just get in the car," I said, throwing the keys at him. He glared at me, to which I returned a cunning smile.

We drove to Samtah, which was about fifteen minutes from our town, after having wasted a quarter of an hour arguing about it.

On the way, I commented on the work that had been done on the car. We listened to songs. Our tastes differed on Arabic songs, but we agreed on the western ones—R&B to be more precise. Then we discussed his studies at college. I asked him about some of my friends who taught there.

"In case you need any help, don't hesitate to talk to them," I advised. However, he wasn't keen on what I was saying. He was, instead, interested in my stories about England, especially about dance clubs. Mostly, he wanted to know if I had made any intimate friendships with any blonde girls. Everybody was interested in the last part, even my own wife, but her interest was of another nature. It was a feminine feeling that I considerately acknowledged, but never dared to explore.

The road seemed empty. A couple of cars passed us using both lanes. Hassan drove rather fast, around 120 kilometres per hour. It didn't bother me. I paid attention to the expansion that had been made to the road. The government planned to construct an international highway from the border of Yemen to the northern borders.

"Do you know that if you go over 120, you'll get fined?" Hassan informed me as he tuned the radio.

"Since when?"

"About two months ago."

"How much is it?"

"Around a hundred riyal, but if you are driving really fast, you will be locked up for a day or two."

"By whom?"

"By the road security police," he continued. "Haven't you noticed the patrol cars in white and green? They came three months after you first left." He was excited because he knew something that I had not been aware of. As I listened to him, I watched the brightly full moon shining over the tree-packed valley.

Suddenly, a huge cloud of sand covered the road in front of us. Hassan panicked, but was able to slow down and stop at the side of the road. We looked at each other with confusion. We saw car lights flash in front of us and three other cars pulled in behind us. In the middle of the road, there were two cars, a red and a white one. There had been a shattering collision. The gravity of the situation left us stunned. In a matter of seconds, our car could have been among the crashed ones.

I rushed out with the other people towards the cars. We approached the white car that was on the side of the road. The sight of it shocked everyone. I believed that none of the passengers would be alive after that. The car was like a piece of paper that had been ferociously folded by an anxious writer. A hand dangled out of a narrow space in the flattened car. The body of an injured youth was stretched out on the ground. The crash had forced him out of the vehicle. He was covered in blood, his *thob* pulled up, exposing his wounded legs. I reached him and he stared at me, speechless. He needed help, yet helpless I stood. We gathered around him. He coughed, but thick blood gushed from his mouth and nose.

"Anyone with a firm heart take him to the hospital," the voice of a chubby man directed us to what should be done. A car was brought and four men carried him up. Whether they were helping him or hurting him, it didn't matter. I was so close that I could hear the splintering of his broken arms as they moved him. I stood there doing nothing; I just watched, disoriented.

After that, we hastened to the red car, leaving the other person behind in the white car. No human hand could get him out of there. Only a machine could saw him out of the steel that clutched greedily to his flesh.

Lots of cars arrived on the scene and people gathered around like a herd of wild dogs finding prey. Shouts of distress were heard every now and then, interrupted with queries about whether anyone was alive. Steam was coming from the car. The whole front was squeezed backwards like it had been powerfully pressed against a wall. Everyone was afraid that the car would catch on fire.

The police had been called, but it would be a while

before they arrived. I didn't think of calling the police; five people had already done that. I looked at Hassan who was nervously quiet. Desiring us to leave, he signaled to me, but a strange feeling forced me to stay. I closely approached the car around which a crowd had gathered. There were two passengers inside. They were trapped in their seats, their heads leaning on their chests as if they were sleeping. Our shouts and bangs didn't bother them. People desperately pulled at the jammed doors. A tall man shouted at us to pull harder, which everyone did. He went to the side and brought a big stone. Running like a cricket player, he smashed the car's rear windshield. The back doors were uselessly opened. Nobody could extract the two boys.

A man managed to make a slight space by pulling at the driver's door. I immediately helped him; with all my might, I pulled. I even tried to push my legs as he pulled, but we sorrowfully yielded to the fact that it was hopeless. In that entire clamor, an eccentric thought came to me, making me feel contempt for myself and all the time I had spent building up my knowledge. I had totally neglected my physical well-being and never thought that I would be in need of it. I stood there, weak—unable to do anything.

The police finally arrived. To my surprise, there were two other cars that swerved off the road when the two cars had collided. Luckily, there were no injuries. I went over to Hassan, who was upset. We stood watching the police and the firefighters do their job. Cars were called on to pass, to keep the road clear. Equipment was brought to extricate the bodies from the cars.

Hassan asked if I still wanted to go to Samtah. It was only three minutes further. I looked at him and saw the panic in his eyes. I told him I would go another time.

As I was getting into the car, a familiar voice came from

behind me, saying, "Welcome, Mr. British." I looked around to reassure myself and it was my friend, Ali. It had been a year since we last met. In spite of the surroundings, we were able to put smiles on our faces. We chatted for a while, saying we would meet later.

At home, Hassan and I gave an exaggerated narration of the accident to the rest of the family.

"My heart is with their mothers," my mother lamented. Only a mother can sympathize with another.

I went to my house to be embraced by my wife who couldn't unreservedly express her emotions in front of my family. I told her about the accident again. Yet I confided to her the contempt I had for myself. I was helpless; I would rather get killed a thousand times than to ever have that feeling again. She calmed me down by reminding me that everyone is required to do the best he can. She kissed me and I brushed her delicate face with my hand. I spotted a black mark on my hand. I scrutinized it, observing the fine, fair edges separating the layers of skin from each other. I showed my wife like a child trying to prove his story wasn't a lie. She examined it, fearing that I might have wounded myself. I felt proud, but I knew in some other village, certain people would show the stains of blood on their clothes and hands. Another person would have to bear a lot of trouble to get the blood washed from his car. I looked at the mark that I wished I could frame and tell Rakan, my son, all about. I wanted to tell him how helpless I was.

"Wash your hands and let's go to the other house. I have cooked supper there," my wife calmly told me. She went to fetch something from inside the bedroom. I washed my hands and went out. I stopped at the erect pillars and looked up at the beautiful moon again. My wife's footsteps called my attention to her presence. She joined in at looking at the moon, the thing I had longed for most in England.

"It is beautiful, isn't it?" she asked.

"Sure, it is, but not as beautiful as you, my dear."

A bashful smile appeared on her lips, and she said, "I am glad you are here tonight."

I tightly held her close to me. I kissed her forehead and nuzzled her long, black hair, and then we went to the other house where I would meet Rakan.

Merciless Bastard

One afternoon, I decided to read the daily newspaper in the vicinity of the front yard of our house. The high concrete wall protected me from the prying eyes of our ancient neighbours. While I was reading, Susana the cat, joined me. The weather seemed to suit her, too. It was a nice day, especially now that the sandstorm season was two weeks behind us. I had had to put up with it for a whole month. I knew it wouldn't be a pleasant time to have a vacation, but I had a whole month left with the family.

A low, yet sharp 'meow' came behind Susana, introducing a small, white kitten. Its head was rather bigger than the normal size. The children insisted on calling him 'The Brain' because he reminded them of a cartoon character on the show they used to watch, in which a mouse wanted to take over the world. Its other three siblings disappeared a week after their birth and it was believed they had been eaten by other stray cats.

'The Brain' he was named. I still remember my first encounter with him. I was invited to a wedding feast one night, thirteen more were ahead of me. I was going to wear a *thob* that I had had tailored for such occasions. To my surprise, I opened the wardrobe to meet The Brain and his siblings struggling in the blood and other disgusting liquids that came with his birth. Unfortunately, the lower part of my *thob* turned out to be a canvas for their gothic artistry. I was so possessed with rage that I wanted to throw him and his mother out of the house, but my wife calmed me down. She even tried to look after them. Everybody in the house roared with laughter when they heard about what had happened. Luckily, Khalid, my young brother, lent me one of his *thobs*. I was amazed that we were almost the same size except that my belly stood out a bit. After returning late at night, my wife welcomed me by mockingly patting my belly and teasingly suggesting that I do some exercises.

Susana, laying on her side in a queenly posture, invited her son to his meal. He stepped forwarded to one of her pinkish nipples and started suckling. She, on the other hand, licked him all over. I looked at her and recalled the way my wife first breastfed our firstborn child, Sami. It was an intriguing, but moving scene. Both her mother and mine were there instructing her. They even held one of her nipples and placed it in Sami's mouth, who, after various attempts, finally knew what he was supposed to do. I wondered if Susana, who'd been living with us for a while, had someone to instruct her on her first delivery.

I continued reading the daily. Most of what the columnists had written was about the effects of the stock market on people. There were a lot of casualties, some had died of heart attacks, others underwent therapy. The psychiatrists seemed to benefit from all of this. I was glad that

I had sold all my shares at the beginning and was satisfied with the money I had made. Yet, everyone was trying to find out who was behind such a lethal drop in the market. I thought most of the people were insane. Imagine someone wagering all his life savings and expecting to profit with twice the money he had paid into the market. Everybody thought they would win a lot of money, but they didn't have the slightest thought of losing. In the end, they had lost everything. We have to lose sometimes in our life, but weeping on what we had clumsily lost doesn't help.

Susana interrupted my reading by brushing herself against my legs. Her thin tail snaked around my left leg. She looked at me with eyes that blinked every time she meowed. I understood what she was trying to say. She wanted me to keep an eye on her son. She thought she could trust me with him.

"Okay, girl, you can go. He'll be safe with me," I said brushing her chin. She replied with a purr, and off she went, leaving the little fellow with me.

I played with him for a while. I pulled a long fine thread from the cushion behind my back and made him chase it around my plastic chair. I smiled every time he laid on his back and unsuccessfully attempted to clap his little paws on the thread. I enjoyed the way he sneaked up on the thread, but I was one step ahead of him all the time.

My mobile phone rang, distracting me from him. My friend, Abdullah, was calling to remind me that tonight was the wedding of our friend, Sultan. He was getting married to a second wife. He had managed to make a fortune on the stock market before the recent crisis. I was on the phone and my eyes were following the young fellow as he hopped around joyfully.

A strange meow declared the arrival of a grey cat that approached, leisurely walking on the wall. I recognized the cat; it had appeared in the house two years ago. Somebody must have thrown the animal near our house, and thus it had dwelt its vicinity. It stopped walking and sat looking at the young fellow. I didn't think that it would be a threat to him, especially as he was a harmless kitten. I was telling Abdullah when he should pick me up when the grey cat suddenly jumped down, increased its speed, and attacked the young kitten. I was shocked and hung on Abdullah.

It had happened so fast. It attacked the defenceless fellow, took hold of his neck within its jaws, quickly snapped it around, and it was done. I ran, hurling my shoes at it with all of my might, but it leapt athletically onto my BMW and over the wall, disappearing from my sight.

I ran back to the little fellow, but he was not breathing. His stomach was still. I tried to move his feeble limbs, but it was no use. He was gone; the cat had killed him. I had failed to protect him.

Seconds later, Susana was back. She was carrying a green grasshopper in her mouth. She approached her son and placed it near him. He was spread motionlessly in front of me. She sniffed him all round. With desperate meows, she tried waking him from his sleep.

She looked at me, but I sat there sulkily, glancing at her young son. She, trying to scold me I thought, meowed at me. I imagined her attempting to speak to me in a sorrowful tone. *But I left him with you*, she would launch. *You couldn't keep an eye on him for such a short time. How could you let this happen to him? I thought I could entrust him to you!* It would add to the drama of the situation if she could express her heavy grievance by scratching my face ferociously with her paws.

I didn't know what took hold of me. Rage? Maybe a desire for vengeance? I couldn't tell. The little fellow didn't do anything wrong. He had harmed no one. Abdullah called, but I didn't pick up. I dashed inside the house and brought out my rifle. I'd just cleaned it two days ago. I was planning to tour the valleys hunting hares and birds. The rifle was loaded so I set off on my quest. I searched furtively. Our house was rather big and had at least two entrances aside from the main one. I looked in the back garden, but there was no trace of the murderer. Everybody in the house anxiously asked me what I was looking for. A sulk was my reply. I even shouted at the children when they attempted to follow me. I seldom did that with them.

Finally, I found my rival. It was laying on the brown grain sacks that had been brought out of storage. Fifty sacks that father was planning to sell at the Monday market. Each one would cost around 250 riyals. I positioned myself in front of the cat. It was resting after its devilish deed. I looked it in the eyes. Mockingly, it looked back, pretending that it hadn't done anything wrong. I stiffened, held my breath, and raised the rifle to shoulder level. I took a final look at the cat and pulled the trigger. The rifle shook, tipping my right shoulder. A faint milky line of smoke danced its way upwards.

The murderer jumped up and fell, plunging its head into the ground. To ease the pain, I thought. Its legs swung quickly. Its tail, like a propeller, rolled over and over till the ninth soul had been pulled out. I stood still, observing all of this. It was dead. I felt somehow pleased. I didn't care about what the others in the house would say. Surprisingly, nobody ran out of the house to see what had happened. I had avenged Susana and her deceased son and that was all that mattered to me. I approached the murderous cat. The bullet had gone right between the eyes as it always did. A dusty line of blood demarcated its two sides. More space was given to the left side, as the line of blood trickled down the right side of the nose. I didn't pay attention to the awfulness of the sight. I looked with complete apathy.

As I was leaving, I heard a faint meow coming from behind the sacks. I bent down to see. To my surprise, I found a small kitten. It was grey with black spots spread all over its thin body. It crawled out and headed towards the dead cat. It went around it, sniffing and meowing in an attempt to make the dead cat respond, but to no effect. Guilt crept into me. I had ended up becoming what its mother had been minutes ago. If I had forgiven the cat, I would have ended up with a meowing mother, but now there was a meowing kitten. I wished all of that had been a dreadful dream. But it wasn't.

I returned to Susana with the orphan kitten. I thought she might accept the idea of a kitten for a kitten. I placed it in front of her. Both meowed at each other. Were they exchanging apologies for the brutality of the grey cat and me? Or were they exchanging condolences? I wondered about this for a while. However, through all of this, I was alert. I didn't want the same accident to happen again. Susana turned out to be more forgiving than I had been. She laid on her side, exposing her nipples to the kitten, who stepped forward and suckled. The offer had been accepted and it was over.

Yet, my job wasn't done. I had to clean up the mess. I took Susana's son and the dead cat, placed them in a brown coverless box and sneaked it out. I left it near old Ahmad Ali's yard. The whole neighbourhood threw its rubbish there. I was lucky. The street was empty; nobody had seen me dispose of the victims of the crime. One thing I was sure of: Ahmad Ali would pass by, look at the litter, then would glance around him quietly. He would adjust thick, dark-framed glasses, slowly scratch the brownish mole on his chin, and finally burst out angrily, "Who's the merciless bastard who killed a cat and its kitten?!"

The Matchmaker

Since the return of her brother Abdullah from the states, Sarah, who was thirteen years younger, had been noticeably ecstatic. Abdullah had completed his Ph.D. in commercial law after seven years of hard study. He was going to teach at the university within a month. For a man of thirty-three, he was successful and everyone in his family was proud of his achievements. His father, a well-known businessman, threw a big party in his honour and bought him a brand new Lexus GS.

Sarah was very fond of Abdullah and she continuously boasted about him in front of her colleagues since the time he had set off to the states. One time she kept showing off in front of her friends the latest version of the iPhone that still hadn't reached the Saudi market yet. "My brother Abdullah sent it to me from America. You see, he is a student there," was the reply to any inquiry about the source of any gifts that she got.

On Thursday night, Sarah prepared tea, coffee, dates,

biscuits, and a chocolate cake. Her humming echoed as she brought the trays from the kitchen to the living room. After everything was set, she turned on the TV and watched the music channel. She danced to the tune of the songs. She, in hilarious and quick wavy moves, shook her bosom voluptuously and twitched her rear. Afterwards, she flung herself onto one of the chairs and treated herself to delicacies she had prepared.

After awhile, Abdullah arrived from work. He had opened an office where he gave legal counselling. Although he was thirty-three, grey hair left a few touches on the sideburns and on his thin, black beard. It was harmonious with his serious and benevolent features. He had an erect fit body and he walked in brisk, short steps. The moment he was seated, Sarah jumped up, sat beside him, and bombarded him with questions about his day. She served him tea and some pieces of biscuits and cake. In fact, she fed him herself.

Their mother came and joined them. Although she was ill, her maternal beauty was still radiant.

"You will make me choke," said Abdullah, his mouth stuffed with biscuits. Yet Sarah continued feeding him. The moment he swallowed a piece of cake, he found a biscuit shoved into his mouth. He laughed helplessly.

While Sarah and her mother enjoyed their time listening to Abdullah's stories about the States and the people there, the doorbell rang. The maid, Sittee, opened the door to let a woman in. She was wearing a black *abaya* embroidered with flowers in a crimson silk thread at the end of the sleeves. The manner in which she dressed would lead one to conclude that she was one of the modern girls of today. The *abaya* she wore was tightened at her slim waist and at her blossoming chest. Her headscarf was worn in a way that allowed a few curls of her dark hair to rest on her delicate, fair forehead. She concealed her face with a transparent veil wrapped over the lower part of her face. Her two mesmerizing eyes, which were demarcated with kohl, were spared from the veil, and left free to enchant the observers.

"Salaam," she greeted them in a cheerful tone as she uncovered her face. Yet she, like a threatened crab hiding in its shell, swiftly put the veil back on when she noticed that a man was on the premises.

It was Norah, Sarah's friend; the two of them had been intimate friends since they were in secondary school. They were used to visiting each other on weekends. They studied in the same department. That night they said they had to work on a project that was supposed to be handed in the week after so they couldn't go window shopping as was their usual habit. Sarah welcomed the girl and they both went upstairs.

The next day after lunch, Abdullah told Sarah that he wanted to speak with her in his room. He asked her to make him some tea. Sarah made the tea and headed to her brother's room. She knocked on the door.

"Come in," Abdullah's deep, calm voice came from behind the door. She entered and found him behind his small desk that was opposite the double bed. He was reading a book, his head resting on both hands.

She placed the mug on the desk and took a glance at the books arranged on shelves behind him. Some were new and others were old. Some she figured out while others left her at a loss. Her brother closed the book after drawing a few lines on one of the pages. He took the mug and sank into his chair.

"How are your studies?" he asked.

"Okay," Sarah replied.

"Your mother told me that you and Norah, your friend who was here last night, are inseparable. And that you are in the same year." Abdullah took a sip from his mug.

Sarah nodded.

"Excellent! To save you time, you know me—I like getting to the point straight away. I am a single man and I'll be turning thirty-four within months. I, thanks to Allah, have managed to gather some money through my stay in the States."

There was no need for Abdullah to continue. Sarah was a clever girl and she knew what her brother was trying to say. He had the intention of getting married and it seemed that her friend had captured his attention. It must have been her eyes.

Yet, what was beyond Sarah's comprehension was her brother's true intentions. She didn't know that he wanted to have an open-minded wife, one who wouldn't embarrass him when travelling outside the Kingdom. During his stay in the States, he had met many people from different Arab countries. He was impressed by the level of freedom some of their women had. They drove cars and were independent. He wanted to show his namesake Abdullah from Kuwait that the women in Saudi Arabia were open-minded and not shamefully covered. In other words, he needed a wife to boast about and to show the world, not to conceal her from it. It was a pity that this dream could only be lived outside his country.

"Last night, your mother gave me hints about the matter," he continued. "But I didn't show any interest. She mentioned one of our relatives, I think her name was Lyla, but I didn't want to appear anxious about the subject. I can't deny that I fancy your friend.

"From the way your mother talked about her, I think she would be the perfect match for me. She would easily fit in as a member of the family. Yet, your mother told me that she wanted me to marry one of uncle's daughters, the one I told you about. So I would really appreciate it if you would help me by giving me your opinion since you have better knowledge of the two girls."

Sarah, who never expected to find herself in such a situation, was bewildered by her brother's request. She never thought her opinion would be of interest to anybody. In fact, she never thought she was to pass judgment on her dearest of friends. She, thinking about Norah, went back their first year in college.

It was Wednesday. Psychology class was over and the girls were coming out of the hall. They were either walking in pairs or in groups. Sarah and Norah were the last to come out. As was their habit, they argued about the issue of being taught through a screen. Because the teacher was a man, the lesson was conducted through a TV set. The girls could only see the teacher's handwriting and sometimes his hands, which they sometimes found tempting.

"El-Shasah's lessons are really dull," Sarah complained as she adjusted the ring on her mobile.

"Well, I don't suppose you want us to get exposed to a foreign man," was Norah's calm reply. The two continued their banter as they headed to the cafeteria. On the way, they discussed the effect that direct contact with the teacher may have on the learning process and how much it would enrich the students' knowledge, a point they always ended up with mutually agreeing on.

"But don't forget," Norah argued. "Some of the girls may try to raise silly topics to embarrass the teacher. You saw how Miss Hind, the supervisor, made one of the girls leave the class last week because she was talking in a flirtatious manner."

"I know, but those girls come to college because they want a piece of paper that says that they have finished their education," Sarah said. "Plus, most of them sit at the back of the hall and either send texts or draw heart shapes on chairs."

The sound of a text message on Norah's mobile interrupted their usual discussion. She read the message and a slight smile appeared on her lips. She passed the mobile to Sarah, who read the message and smiled in return.

"Looks like he is really deep in love, girl," Sarah said,

pinching Norah's arm. The two of them giggled as they reread the message.

When they arrived at the cafeteria, it wasn't crowded. It was a big hall that had round tables placed randomly, with four chairs circling each table. Some plastic plants sat in the corners and artificial flowers hung on the walls. The windows were covered with dark sticky labels so nobody could see what was inside. The two ordered coffee and sat at a table at the end of the hall. Sarah always insisted on sitting at that table every time they came here.

"I can't understand your insistence on sitting at this table every time we come here," Norah objected.

"Nevermind! Just tell me what you're going to do with this, what's his name?" Sarah asked as she stirred sugar in her cup.

"His name is Ahmad. And what I am going to do with him will not go beyond the rules."

"Not bad! You're picking up quickly. I'm beginning to be afraid of you, you heartbreaker," Sarah said with a cunning smile. "Drink quickly, we don't want to be late for history class."

During the history lecture, things went differently. The teacher, Miss Nouha, never allowed any naughtiness to happen in her class. In fact, she never allowed anyone to come inside once her class was in session. The class was packed with students. The girls had difficulty walking through rows that barely existed anyhow. The hall was designed to encompass thirty students yet the section had forty-five. The teacher lectured while the girls hunched over their notebooks writing everything she uttered. Every five minutes, they raised their heads to see what Miss Nouha generously scribbled on the board.

After class, the two girls agreed to meet on the weekend and see what mischief they could scheme up to kill their boredom.

Their friendship had started when they were in secondary school. Norah's family moved into the neighbourhood that Sarah lived in. Of course, nobody knew who moved in or out of the neighbourhood due to the nature of city life. However, it was different when it came to school. Norah, eventually, came to be known as the 'new girl' for a short period of time. During her first weeks at school, she didn't make any close friendships. She was quiet and sat by herself during the lunch break. Most of the girls didn't like her because she was one of the bright students. They thought she was arrogant.

Sarah, on the other hand, was popular in school and all the girls liked her. Everyone wanted to be friends with her. She was naughty and full of mischief. She always bothered the teachers with questions that turned out to be puns. Whether it was fate or mere coincidence, Norah found herself sitting beside Sarah. Nothing happened between them except a brief introduction with typical questions: *What's your name? Where are you from? What does your father do?*

Time passed and the two didn't talk much to each other. Sarah made a few jokes about Norah to make the whole class laugh. One day, the class was taken by a surprise inspection. The headmistress came to search all the girls' bags. Sarah was shocked. She had brought a few fashion magazines to show her friends. The girls usually exchanged tales and magazines at school. Sarah thought her exchanging days were over. The headmistress checked the back rows and the school teacher checked the front ones. Sarah was cornered; she didn't know what to do with the magazines. She knew that the teacher wanted to catch her breaking any of the school's rules. The teacher would enjoy punishing Sarah for all the trouble she had caused her in class.

When Sarah found there was no way out, she decided to reveal her magazines to the teacher who was busy checking Norah's bag. Being the top student in the class, Norah was beyond suspicion. The teacher took a swift look at Norah's bag and then turned towards Sarah.

Sarah, who was determined not to give the teacher the slightest chance to boast about catching her red-handed, was going to place the magazines on the desk. Suddenly, she felt Norah tugging on her uniform. Norah gestured to her to pass the magazines. Sarah did and was saved from inspection. It was so that the two had become friends. In fact, their friendship expanded to reach their families. The two fathers, being businessmen, found common interest between them, and their mother's became best friends.

At night, Norah visited Sarah. Her bedroom was large and had its own bathroom. The walls were covered with green wallpaper with drawings of roses on it. A soft evening breeze moved the curtains of a large window that offered a good view of the back garden, in which a few roses grew. Arabic music echoed around the room, accompanied by the chuckles of the two girls who were hunched over their mobiles.

Norah was typing swiftly and Sarah was leaning over her shoulder, dictating. They had found a new prey in one of the chat apps. They considered it a game to waste their leisure time on. They would usually find someone in a chat and flirt with him. The whole flirting game was Sarah's idea. Compared to Sarah, Norah was still an amateur. Sarah had a strong character and a sharp mind. She cleverly played with boys' feelings. They would tell him their names, which they made up, and say he was a 'cool guy,' open-minded and not like the others that they had met so far, guys with intentions other than honest friendship. They would continue flirting with the dupe and would ask him for iTunes cards. They would even go so far as to ask him to send some pictures of himself. In return, they would send a picture of a monkey or a cat. After the desperate lover would send the code of the cards, the girls would ask him to meet them at a certain shopping mall and to carry a rose as a distinguishing mark. However, the girls would never turn up and would make the excuse that they weren't able to go because their brothers had insisted on accompanying them. The two of them had been entertaining themselves that way through all the weekends they claimed to have spent studying. Even their parents were glad the girls were close friends. "They are killing themselves studying," Norah's mother would say in her high-pitched voice.

After the two girls had finished their entertainment that night, they settled down with fashion magazines, which Sarah always kept on the side table. They looked for any new perfumes that might intrigue them.

"I want to tell you something," Norah said with slight hesitation.

Sarah, who was skimming a magazine, told her to say what was on her mind.

"I met Ahmad before I came here," Norah murmured.

Sarah's eyes went wide and she burst out, "Are you sane?"

Norah was quiet as she stared at a few toys arranged on a bookshelf. Beside them, there was a small, red heart-shaped pillow.

"Where did you meet him?" Sarah asked.

"At El-Fisalia Tower."

"Did he ask to meet you?"

"Yes."

"Tell me all about this unexpected stunt."

Norah had met Ahmad at a cafe. According to her, he was nice and very polite. He just wanted to talk to her. Norah described how she enjoyed the sweetness of the adventure. She also told Sarah about the love poems he recited, ones he thought would best describe Norah's eyes.

"He kept praising my eyes...saying they're heavenly orbs," Norah said excitedly.

"I hope you didn't give him a full view of the heavenly galaxy," Sarah replied.

Sarah thought that she was being harsh with her friend so she decided to be more easy-going about it. However, she warned her not to get carried away with her secret lover. Unlike Norah, Sarah never agreed to meet with any of the boys she flirted with. She never trembled to the tenderness of their words and always lied about her feelings.

"Be careful! Don't let him touch you or see your face, no matter what," Sarah said firmly to her friend. "Here men only have one sick feeling towards us girls. They approach you with all the compassion in the world until they seize their truly desired quest. Norah, be alert to anything he says to you because he doesn't mean a word he is saying."

"But he is a nice person," Norah said in defense.

"They are all nice at the beginning."

"No, Ahmad is different."

"What makes you so sure?"

"I can tell by the way he talks to me."

"Yeah, sure."

"Why are you saying that?"

"Because you don't know how to deal with boys."

"What makes you think so?! I'm not a little girl!"

"You're not, but you're naïve."

"I'm not! You're saying that because you are jealous."

Sarah, offended by her friend's remark, said, "I just dumped three boys this month. How many have you known so far?"

The two of them parted that night angry with the other. They didn't meet for a couple of weekends. They felt they needed to stay away from each other until the tide was calm. They agreed to forget about the whole flirting game. The midterm exams that were starting in a week managed to wash away the remains of the slight disagreement and things went back to their usual course.

During that short period, Norah skipped a few of their weekend meetings. She always apologized, saying that either relatives were visiting or she was visiting them. Sarah trusted her friend and never thought Norah was trying to avoid her. The intelligence that Sarah didn't possess at that time was that her friend had lied to her.

Norah continued meeting her alleged lover. The ecstasy of the adventure made her get carried away with exploring the world of forbidden romance. Her lover, Ahmad, succeeded in charming her with his calm, soothing praises. He captured her heart with his words, which revealed his long experience in the field of seduction. He managed with well-planned steps to lure her into his usual trap. All he had needed was to be patient. He sweetly kissed her hand, which made her tremble with a fearful delight. Then she enjoyed the electrifying kiss on the cheek. Finally, she was all set to dissolve when her delicate lips met Ahmad's firm ones, lips that were crowned with a thinly trimmed mustache.

Norah thought she was living in a world of happiness. There was nothing that a girl her age needed more than someone who would care for her. Norah longed for Ahmad's kisses and words. She slept embracing her pillow, imagining it was him.

She hid the gifts he sent her in the wardrobe. She read his letters and poems every night. Although she knew that what she was doing was forbidden, she continued doing it. She cared less about her family, who didn't pay any attention to her anyhow. Nobody cared about her. Her father rarely asked about her, her brothers didn't even look at her, and her mother was always busy visiting friends.

However, to think happiness can be eternal was only a dream that Norah was living in. The time came when sweet delusion was to turn into a nightmare. Her blind trust of Ahmad caused her to commit a slight mistake, the kind that most of the adventurous and savvy girls usually didn't commit. Such a mistake lead to a complicated consequence. Poor Norah had fallen for what was known as the oldest trick in the book.

One week Sarah noticed that her friend was absent for two days and whenever she called Norah on her mobile, she found that it was switched off. She then called Norah's mother who informed her that Norah was ill and in the hospital. She was to be out in a day or two. Yet the doctor had advised Norah not to receive any visitors while she was in the hospital.

Sarah was upset to find out so late. *Last week, she was very cheerful. What could have happened to her?* Sarah asked herself after the phone call.

Sarah and her mother went to visit Norah when she returned home from the hospital. They were welcomed by Norah's mother. Although her daughter was ill, she was cheerful. They sat in the women's guest room where they drank coffee and tea and ate dates. Norah's father wasn't at the house; he was still at his office.

"Since the stock market business started, we never see much of him," Norah's mother said. "Even Yasser and Sa'ad have decided to join their father."

Sarah's mother, who had been doing most of the talking, inquired about Norah's health.

"Stress," Norah's mother replied, handing her guest a tea cup. "The doctor says she has been under stress lately and she needs some rest. The examinations are wearing them out. Look at your daughter, dear—I think she lost weight."

Sarah blushed, taking it as a compliment. She had managed to lose two kilograms after a three-month diet.

"I don't know what the use of their studying is. A woman should be looking after her husband and children,"

Norah's mother said. Sarah's mother disagreed with her friend on that issue. Sarah took advantage of that moment and said that she wanted to go and see Norah.

Norah's room was small and cozy. It didn't have many decorations in it. Norah was in her bed and she was pale. She had lost the glow in her eyes. They were red from crying and her face could be best described as *tear-stained*. She was weak and her voice could barely be heard.

Sarah couldn't believe that the person lying in bed was her friend, Norah. She sat beside her friend, who tried to put on a weak smile. She stroked Norah's hand, hoping that she would become better soon.

When Sarah asked about the reason behind her illness, Norah wept and covered her face with a pillow. Sarah realized that this wasn't a good start so she tried to calm her friend down.

"The doctor said you shouldn't upset yourself," Sarah said, stroking her friend's hand again. "If you don't stop crying, your condition will become worse and everyone will say that I should stay away from you." Sarah continued trying to cheer up her friend.

Norah kept saying, "Forgive me! I should have listened to you."

Sarah didn't know what her friend was talking about. She tried to calm her down by telling her that she forgave her. She poured her a glass of water from a pitcher that was on the table beside the bed. She held it out to Norah, who gulped from the glass; her loud breathing was hushed every time she swallowed.

Taking into consideration Norah's condition, Sarah told her that it wasn't necessary to say anything at that moment. Yet Norah was determined to tell her what had happened to her. Norah started narrating her story in a shaky voice marked with bitter regret and humility.

"I continued meeting Ahmad even though you and I had

agreed to stop the game," Norah said. "Every time I told you I was visiting relatives, I would spend it with him. He was very considerate to me and never asked me anything that would offend me. He seduced me with the most passionate words that he whispered in my ear, like he was pretending to tell me a secret. He bought me gifts and even composed poems describing his love to me. He used to drive me around Riyadh and we would go to parks and malls and we even ate at restaurants many times. I felt that he was my soul mate. I loved and trusted every word he said. I even made him kiss me.

"However, one day he told me that he wanted to propose to me and that he was going to discuss it with his father, of whose approval he was sure. I was so overtaken with joy that I couldn't doubt anything he said after that. He asked me if I would like to see the flat that we would be living in after we married. I hesitated at first, but because I trusted him, I agreed. He took me to his apartment and there..."

Norah started moaning over those words and Sarah embraced her firmly. She didn't need to finish her story. She knew exactly what her friend was trying to tell Norah—she wasn't a virgin anymore. She had every right to feel unhappy, but if her family found out, they might feel she had no right to live.

"He said he loved me," Norah cried in a faint, upset voice. "I tried to call him many times, but he didn't answer. I kept on until one day he answered. All the compassion he used to welcome me with was replaced by contempt and rudeness. I asked him why he hadn't come back to ask for my hand and he said he had changed his mind. He said I wasn't the girl for him. He told me that he couldn't trust a girl who cheated on her family. I told him I did it because I loved him, but he said he stopped loving me after that because he thought I was easy. He even said that I was a whore..."

Sarah hushed Norah by placing her hand over her friend's mouth. "It's too late to feel sorry even though you might think it helps," Sarah said firmly. "But being sorry won't get us any place. Leave everything to me. I'm the one who got you into this mess and I'm responsible for getting you out of it."

Sarah knew a gynecologist who worked in one of the private hospitals. She was a patient because she used to suffer from severe period pain. She, for extra money, would make Norah be her old self again. It was a matter of a simple surgery and she would be as good as new. As for confidentiality, it was one of the merits of that doctor.

Time passed. Norah got over that dreadful incident. She returned to her merry self and forgot all about what had happened. Her friendship with Sarah was stronger than before.

One day while they were talking in the college cafeteria, crowded with girls, Norah raised the issue again.

"Do you think I am vile?" she asked.

Sarah was peeping through the window. She was looking outside through an area that she had managed to scratch off the window's surface. She observed the sparrows on the trees outside the college walls. She looked at cars as they passed. Yet her interest was most captured by a tall construction site, which was to be a shopping mall three blocks from the college. She always wondered about the builders, who appeared like ants on a large, glazed ant farm. She imagined the heat of the burning summer sun on their skin; and the sweat that covered their bodies and foreheads which they wiped at with their strong, hairy arms.

When she heard her friend's question, she turned to her with a caring look, and said, "No, you're not. You're my best friend."

Norah smiled back and they both sat quietly and drank their tea.

Two years had passed since that incident and nobody knew about it except the two friends. Yet Sarah found herself facing the ultimate dilemma. Her brother, whom she cherished the most, was asking her opinion concerning her friend. It was an unpleasant conundrum she found herself in. It wasn't that complicated—it was a matter of loyalty. Whom should she be faithful to? She had to choose between her friend and her brother, who didn't know a thing.

It didn't take Sarah long to make up her mind.

"I think our cousin, Lyla, is the perfect match for you. She is an experienced woman and an excellent cook. She is also very beautiful. Mother likes her and so do I," she advised her brother.

"Very well," Abdullah said. "I shall discuss it with mother when the time is appropriate. I hope this stays between the two of us. Oh, please don't bring the subject to your friend!" He gave her leave. She left and he retired to his book.

Mohammed Sumili was born and raised in a small village in the Jazan province in the southern region of Saudi Arabia. He is the father of two children and is currently pursuing his PhD in English at the University of Texas Arlington. He holds a Bachelor of Education in Arts (English Language) from King Khaled University, Saudi Arabia and a Master of Arts in English studies from the University of Exeter, UK. He teaches English at the University of Jazan in Saudi Arabia. He writes fiction and poetry and sometimes short scripts. His first novella, *Memories Resurrected*, was published by Arabesque Publishers in 2010. He has contributed some of his shorter fiction to {stet}, the creative writing journal of UT Arlington's English Department, as well as to *Texas's Emerging Writers: An Anthology of Fiction* (Z Publishing House, 2018). In his free time, he enjoys watching movies and debating with his friends.